Aubrey Beardsley, Ernest Christopher Dowson

The Pierrot of the minute : a dramatic phantasy in one act

Aubrey Beardsley, Ernest Christopher Dowson

The Pierrot of the minute : a dramatic phantasy in one act

ISBN/EAN: 9783337304614

Printed in Europe, USA, Canada, Australia, Japan

Cover: Foto ©Andreas Hilbeck / pixelio.de

More available books at **www.hansebooks.com**

The Pierrot of the Minute

A DRAMATIC PHANTASY
IN ONE ACT

Written by

ERNEST DOWSON

With a Frontispiece, Initial Letter, Vignette, and Cul-de-lampe by

AUBREY BEARDSLEY

LONDON

ROYAL ARCADE W

MDCCCXCVII

THE CHARACTERS

A MOON MAIDEN

PIERROT

THE SCENE

A glade in the Parc du Petit Trianon. In the centre a Doric temple with steps coming down the stage. On the left a little Cupid on a pedestal. Twilight.

(Pierrot enters with his hands full of lilies. He is
burdened with a little basket. He stands gazing at the
Temple and the Statue.)

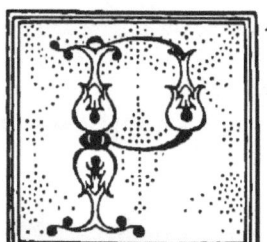

PIERROT.

My journey's end! This surely is the
glade
Which I was promised: I have well
obeyed!
A clue of lilies was I bid to find,
Where the green alleys most obscurely wind;

Where tall oaks darkliest canopy o'erhead,
And moss and violet make the softest bed ;
Where the path ends, and leagues behind me lie
The gleaming courts and gardens of Versailles;
The lilies streamed before me, green and white ;
I gathered, following : they led me right,
To the bright temple and the sacred grove :
This is, in truth, the very shrine of Love !

> (He gathers together his flowers and lays them at
> the foot of Cupid's statue ; then he goes timidly
> up the first steps of the temple and stops.)

Pierrot.   It is so solitary, I grow afraid.

Is there no priest here, no devoted maid ?

Is there no oracle, no voice to speak,

Interpreting to me the word I seek ?

> (A very gentle music of lutes floats out from the
> temple. Pierrot starts back ; he shows extreme
> surprise ; then he returns to the foreground, and
> crouches down in rapt attention until the music ceases.
> His face grows puzzled and petulant.)

Pierrot.   Too soon ! too soon ! in that enchanting strain,

Days yet unlived, I almost lived again :

It almost taught me that I most would know—
Why am I here, and why am I Pierrot?

(Absently he picks up a lily which has fallen to
the ground, and repeats :)

Pierrot. Why came I here, and why am I Pierrot?
That music and this silence both affright;
Pierrot can never be a friend of night.
I never felt my solitude before—
Once safe at home, I will return no more.
Yet the commandment of the scroll was plain;
While the light lingers let me read again.

(He takes a scroll from his bosom and reads :)

Pierrot. " *He loves to-night who never loved before ;*
Who ever loved, to-night shall love once more."
I never loved! I know not what love is.
I am so ignorant—but what is this?
(Reads) " *Who would adventure to encounter Love*
Must rest one night within this hallowed grove.
Cast down thy lilies, which have led thee on,
Before the tender feet of Cupidon."

Thus much is done, the night remains to me.
Well, Cupidon, be my security!
Here is more writing, but too faint to read.

(He puzzles for a moment, then casts the scroll down).

Pierrot.   Hence, vain old parchment.   I have learnt thy rede!

(He looks round uneasily, starts at his shadow; then discovers his basket with glee.   He takes out a flask of wine, pours it into a glass, and drinks.)

Pierrot.   *Courage, mon Ami!*   I shall never miss
Society with such a friend as this.
How merrily the rosy bubbles pass,
Across the amber crystal of the glass.
I had forgotten you.   Methinks this quest
Can wake no sweeter echo in my breast.

(Looks round at the statue, and starts).

Pierrot.   Nay, little god!   forgive.   I did but jest.

(He fills another glass, and pours it upon the statue).

Pierrot.   This libation, Cupid, take,
    With the lilies at thy feet;
Cherish Pierrot for their sake
    Send him visions strange and sweet,
While he slumbers at thy feet.
    Only love kiss him awake!
    Only love kiss him awake!

(Slowly falls the darkness, soft music plays, while Pierrot gathers together fern and foliage into a rough couch at the foot of the steps which lead to the Temple d'Amour. Then he lies down upon it, having made his prayer. It is night.)

Pierrot.   (Softly.)
Music, more music, far away and faint:
It is an echo of mine heart's complaint.
Why should I be so musical and sad?
I wonder why I used to be so glad?
In single glee I chased blue butterflies,
Half butterfly myself, but not so wise,
For they were twain, and I was only one.
Ah me! how pitiful to be alone.
My brown birds told me much, but in mine ear
They never whispered this—I learned it here:

The soft wood sounds, the rustlings in the breeze,
Are but the stealthy kisses of the trees.
Each flower and fern in this enchanted wood
Leans to her fellow, and is understood ;
The eglantine, in loftier station set,
Stoops down to woo the maidly violet.
In gracile pairs the very lilies grow :
None is companionless except Pierrot.
Music, more music ! how its echoes steal
Upon my senses with unlooked for weal.
Tired am I, tired, and far from this lone glade
Seems mine old joy in rout and masquerade.
Sleep cometh over me, now will I prove,
By Cupid's grace, what is this thing called love.

        (Sleeps.)

        (There is more music of lutes for an interval,
    during which a bright radiance, white and cold, streams
    from the temple upon the face of Pierrot. Presently a
    Moon Maiden steps out of the temple ; she descends and
    stands over the sleeper.)

The Lady.   Who is this mortal
                    Who ventures to-night
                To woo an immortal,

Cold, cold the moon's light,
For sleep at this portal,
Bold lover of night.
Fair is the mortal
In soft, silken white,
Who seeks an immortal.
Ah, lover of night,
Be warned at the portal,
And save thee in flight!

(She stoops over him : Pierrot stirs in his sleep.)

Pierrot.   (Murmuring.)
Forget not, Cupid.   Teach me all thy lore :
" *He loves to-night who never loved before.*"

The Lady.   Unwitting boy ! when, be it soon or late,
What Pierrot ever has escaped his fate ?
What if I warned him !   He might yet evade,
Through the long windings of this verdant glade ;
Seek his companions in the blither way,
Which, else, must be as lost as yesterday.
So might he still pass some unheeding hours
In the sweet company of birds and flowers.

How fair he is, with red lips formed for joy,
As softly curved as those of Venus' boy.
Methinks his eyes, beneath their silver sheaves,
Rest tranquilly like lilies under leaves.
Arrayed in innocence, what touch of grace
Reveals the scion of a courtly race?
Well, I will warn him, though, I fear, too late—
What Pierrot ever has escaped his fate?
But, see, he stirs, new knowledge fires his brain,
And Cupid's vision bids him wake again.
Dione's Daughter! but how fair he is,
Would it be wrong to rouse him with a kiss?

(She stoops down and kisses him, then withdraws
into the shadow.)

Pierrot.   (Rubbing his eyes.)
Celestial messenger! remain, remain;
Or, if a vision, visit me again!
What is this light, and whither am I come
To sleep beneath the stars so far from home?

(Rises slowly to his feet).

Pierrot.   Stay, I remember this is Venus' Grove,
         And I am hither come to encounter——

The Lady.   (Coming forward, but veiled.)
                                    Love !

                  (In ecstacy, throwing himself at her feet.)

Pierrot.   Then have I ventured and encountered Love ?

The Lady.   Not yet, rash boy ! and, if thou wouldst be wise,
         Return unknowing ; he is safe who flies.

Pierrot.   Never, sweet lady, will I leave this place
         Until I see the wonder of thy face.
         Goddess or Naiad ! lady of this Grove,
         Made mortal for a night to teach me love,
         Unveil thyself, although thy beauty be
         Too luminous for my mortality.

The Lady.   (Unveiling.)
         Then, foolish boy, receive at length thy will :
         Now knowest thou the greatness of thine ill.

Pierrot.   Now have I lost my heart, and gained my goal.

The Lady.   Didst thou not read the warning on the scroll?

               (Picking up the parchment.)

Pierrot.   I read it all, as on this quest I fared,
         Save where it was illegible and hard.

The Lady.   Alack! poor scholar, wast thou never taught
         A little knowledge serveth less than naught?
         Hadst thou perused——but, stay, I will explain
         What was the writing which thou didst disdain.
 (Reads)   " *Au Petit Trianon*, at night's full noon,
         Mortal, beware the kisses of the moon!
         Whoso seeks her she gathers like a flower—
         He gives a life, and only gains an hour."

Pierrot.   (Laughing recklessly.)
         Bear me away to thine enchanted bower,
         All of my life I venture for an hour.

The Lady.   Take up thy destiny of short delight;
         I am thy lady for a summer's night.
         Lift up your viols, maidens of my train,

And work such havoc on this mortal's brain
That for a moment he may touch and know
Immortal things, and be full Pierrot.
White music, Nymphs! Violet and Eglantine!
To stir his tired veins like magic wine.
What visitants across his spirit glance,
Lying on lilies, while he watch me dance?
Watch, and forget all weary things of earth,
All memories and cares, all joy and mirth,
While my dance wooes him, light and rythmical,
And weaves his heart into my coronal.
Music, more music for his soul's delight:
Love is his lady for a summer's night.

(Pierrot reclines, and gazes at her while she dances.
The dance finished, she beckons to him: he rises
dreamily, and stands at her side.)

Pierrot.   Whence came, dear Queen, such magic melody?

The Lady.   Pan made it long ago in Arcady.

Pierrot.   I heard it long ago, I know not where,
As I knew thee, or ever I came here.

But I forget all things—my name and race,
All that I ever knew except thy face.
Who art thou, lady?   Breathe a name to me,
That I may tell it like a rosary.
Thou, whom I sought, dear Dryad of the trees,
How art thou designate—art thou Heart's-Ease ?

The Lady.   Waste not the night in idle questioning,
Since Love departs at dawn's awakening.

Pierrot.   Nay, thou art right ; what recks thy name or state,
Since thou art lovely and compassionate.
Play out thy will on me : I am thy lyre.

The Lady.   I am to each the face of his desire.

Pierrot.   I am not Pierrot, but Venus' dove,
Who craves a refuge on the breast of love.

The Lady.   What wouldst thou of the maiden of the moon ?
Until the cock crow I may grant thy boon.

Pierrot.   Then, sweet Moon Maiden, in some magic car,

Wrought wondrously of many a homeless star—
Such must attend thy journeys through the skies,—
Drawn by a team of milk-white butterflies,
Whom, with soft voice and music of thy maids,
Thou urgest gently through the heavenly glades ;
Mount me beside thee, bear me far away
From the low regions of the solar day ;
Over the rainbow, up into the moon,
Where is thy palace and thine opal throne ;
There on thy bosom——

The Lady.   Too ambitious boy !
I did but promise thee one hour of joy.
This tour thou plannest, with a heart so light,
Could hardly be completed in a night.
Hast thou no craving less remote than this ?

Pierrot.   Would it be impudent to beg a kiss ?

The Lady.   I say not that : yet prithee have a care !
Often audacity has proved a snare.
How wan and pale do moon-kissed roses grow—
Dost thou not fear my kisses, Pierrot ?

Pierrot   As one who faints upon the Libyan plain
   Fears the oasis which brings life again !

The Lady.   Where far away green palm trees seem to stand
   May be a mirage of the wreathing sand,

Pierrot.   Nay, dear enchantress, I consider naught,
   Save mine own ignorance, which would be taught.

The Lady.   Dost thou persist ?

Pierrot.   I do entreat this boon !

   (She bends forward, their lips meet : she withdraws
   with a petulant shiver. She utters a peal of clear
   laughter.)

The Lady.   Why art thou pale, fond lover of the moon ?

Pierrot.   Cold are thy lips, more cold than I can tell ;
   Yet would I hang on them, thine icicle !
   Cold is thy kiss, more cold than I could dream
   Arctus sits, watching the Boreal stream :
   But with its frost such sweetness did conspire

That all my veins are filled with running fire ;
Never I knew that life contained such bliss
As the divine completeness of a kiss.

The Lady. Apt scholar! so love's lesson has been taught.
Warning, as usual, has gone for naught.

Pierrot. Had all my schooling been of this soft kind,
To play the truant I were less inclined.
Teach me again !   I am a sorry dunce—
I never knew a task by conning once.

The Lady. Then come with me ! below this pleasant shrine
Of Venus we will presently recline,
Until birds' twitter beckon me away
To mine own home, beyond the milky-way.
I will instruct thee, for I deem as yet
Of Love thou knowest but the alphabet.

Pierrot. In its sweet grammar I shall grow most wise,
If all its rules be written in thine eyes.

(The lady sits upon a step of the temple, and Pierrot
leans upon his elbow at her feet, regarding her.)

Pierrot.   Sweet contemplation ! how my senses yearn
To be thy scholar always, always learn.
Hold not so high from me thy radiant mouth,
Fragrant with all the spices of the South ;
Nor turn, O sweet ! thy golden face away,
For with it goes the light of all my day.
Let me peruse it, till I know by note
Each line of it, like music, note by rote ;
Raise thy long lashes, Lady ! smile again :
These studies profit me.

(Taking her hand.)

The Lady.   Refrain, refrain !

Pierrot.   (With passion.)
I am but studious, so do not stir ;
Thou art my star, I thine astronomer !
Geometry was founded on thy lip.

(Kisses her hand.)

The Lady.   This attitude becomes not scholarship !
Thy zeal I praise ; but, prithee, not so fast,
Nor leave the rudiments until the last.
Science applied is good, but t'were a schism

To study such before the catechism.
Bear thee more modestly, while I submit
Some easy problems to confirm thy wit.

Pierrot. In all humility my mind I pit
Against her problems which would test my wit.

The Lady.   (Questioning him from a little book bound deliciously
in vellum.)
                    What is Love ?
                Is it a folly,
                Is it mirth, or melancholy ?
                Joys above,
                Are there many, or not any ?
                What is love ?

Pierrot.   (Answering in a very humble attitude of scholarship.)
                If you please,
                A most sweet folly !
                Full of mirth and melancholy :
                Both of these !
                In its sadness worth all gladness,
                If you please !

The Lady.   Prithee where,
                    Goes Love a-hiding?
                    Is he long in his abiding
                        Anywhere?
                    Can you bind him when you find him;
                        Prithee, where?

Pierrot.   With spring days
                    Love comes and dallies:
                    Upon the mountains, through the valleys
                        Lie Love's ways.
                    Then he leaves you and deceives you
                        In spring days.

The Lady. Thine answers please me: 'tis thy turn to ask.
        To meet thy questioning be now my task.

Pierrot.   Since I know thee, dear Immortal,
                Is my heart become a blossom,
                To be worn upon thy bosom.
                When thou turn me from this portal,
                Whither shall I, hapless mortal,
                Seek love out and win again
                Heart of me that thou retain?

The Lady.   In and out the woods and valleys,
                     Circling, soaring like a swallow,
                     Love shall flee and thou shalt follow :
                     Though he stops awhile and dallies,
                     Never shalt thou stay his malice !
                     Moon-kissed mortals seek in vain
                     To possess their hearts again !

Pierrot.   Tell me, Lady, shall I never
                     Rid me of this grievous burden !
                     Follow Love and find his guerdon
                     In no maiden whatsoever ?
                     Wilt thou hold my heart for ever ?
                     Rather would I thine forget,
                     In some earthly Pierrette !

The Lady.   Thus thy fate, whate'er thy will is !
                     Moon-struck child, go seek my traces
                     Vainly in all mortal faces !
                     In and out among the lilies,
                     Court each rural Amaryllis :
                     Seek the signet of Love's hand
                     In each courtly Corisande !

Pierrot.   Now, verily, sweet maid, of school I tire:
            These answers are not such as I desire.

The Lady.   Why art thou sad?

Pierrot.   I dare not tell.

The Lady.   (Caressingly.)
                                              Come, say!

Pierrot.   Is love all schooling, with no time to play?

The Lady.   Though all love's lessons be a holiday,
            Yet I will humour thee: what wouldst thou play?

Pierrot.   What are the games that small moon-maids enjoy,
            Or is their time all spent in staid employ?

The Lady.   Sedate they are, yet games they much enjoy:
            They skip with stars, the rainbow is their toy.

Pierrot.   That is too hard!

The Lady.   For mortal's play.

Pierrot.   What then?

The Lady. Teach me some pastime from the world of men.

Pierrot. I have it, maiden

The Lady.   Can it soon be taught?

Pierrot. A simple game, I learnt it at the Court.
I sit by thee.

The Lady.   But, prithee, not so near.

Pierrot. That is essential, as will soon appear.
Lay here thine hand, which cold night dews anoint,
Washing its white——

The Lady.   Now is this to the point?

Pierrot. Prithee, forbear!   Such is the game's design.

The Lady. Here is my hand.

Pierrot.   I cover it with mine.

c

The Lady.   What must I next ?

(They play.)

Pierrot.   Withdraw.

The Lady.   It goes too fast.

(They continue playing, until Pierrot catches her hand.)

Pierrot.   (Laughing.)
Tis done.   I win my forfeit at the last.

(He tries to embrace her.   She escapes; he chases her round the stage ; she eludes him).   •

The Lady.   Thou art not quick enough.   Who hopes to catch
A moon-beam, must use twice as much despatch.

Pierrot.   (Sitting down sulkily.)
I grow aweary, and my heart is sore.
Thou dost not love me ; I will play no more.

(He buries his face in his hands: the lady stands over him.)

The Lady.   What is this petulance ?

Pierrot.   'Tis quick to tell—
Thou hast but mocked me.

The Lady.   Nay ! I love thee well !

Pierrot.   Repeat those words, for still within my breast
A whisper warns me they are said in jest.

The Lady.   I jested not : at daybreak I must go,
Yet loving thee far better than thou know.

Pierrot.   Then, by this altar, and this sacred shrine,
Take my sworn troth, and swear thee wholly mine !
The gods have wedded mortals long ere this.

The Lady.   There was enough betrothal in my kiss.
What need of further oaths ?

Pierrot.   That bound not thee !

The Lady. Peace! since I tell thee that it may not be.
　　　　　But sit beside me whilst I soothe thy bale
　　　　　With some moon fancy or celestial tale.

Pierrot. Tell me of thee, and that dim, happy place
　　　　　Where lies thine home, with maidens of thy race!

The Lady.　　　　　　(Seating herself.)
　　　　　Calm is it yonder, very calm; the air
　　　　　For mortals' breath is too refined and rare;
　　　　　Hard by a green lagoon our palace rears
　　　　　Its dome of agate through a myriad years.
　　　　　A hundred chambers its bright walls enthrone,
　　　　　Each one carved strangely from a precious stone.
　　　　　Within the fairest, clad in purity,
　　　　　Our mother dwelleth immemorially:
　　　　　Moon-calm, moon-pale, with moon stones on her gown
　　　　　The floor she treads with little pearls is sown;
　　　　　She sits upon a throne of amethysts,
　　　　　And orders mortal fortunes as she lists;
　　　　　I, and my sisters, all around her stand,
　　　　　And, when she speaks, accomplish her demand.

Pierrot. Methought grim Clotho and her sisters twain

With shrivelled fingers spun this web of bane!

The Lady. Their's and my mother's realm is far apart;
Her's is the lustrous kingdom of the heart,
And dreamers all, and all who sing and love,
Her power acknowledge, and her rule approve.

Pierrot. Me, even me, she hath led into this grove.

The Lady. Yea, thou art one of hers! But, ere this night,
Often I watched my sisters take their flight
Down heaven's stairway of the clustered stars
To gaze on mortals through their lattice bars;
And some in sleep they woo with dreams of bliss
Too shadowy to tell, and some they kiss.
But all to whom they come, my sisters say,
Forthwith forget all joyance of the day,
Forget their laughter and forget their tears,
And dream away with singing all their years—
Moon-lovers always!

(She sighs.)

Pierrot.   Why art sad, sweet Moon?
(Laughing.)

The Lady.   For this, my story, grant me now a boon.

Pierrot.   I am thy servitor.

The Lady.   Would, then, I knew
More of the earth, what men and women do.

Pierrot.   I will explain.

The Lady.   Let brevity attend
Thy wit, for night approaches to its end.

Pierrot.   Once was I a page at Court, so trust in me :
That's the first lesson of society.

The Lady.   Society ?

Pierrot.   I mean the very best
Pardy ! thou wouldst not hear about the rest.
I know it not, but am a *petit maître*
At rout and festival and *bal champêtre.*
But since example be instruction's ease,
Let's play the thing.—Now, Madame, if you please!

(He helps her to rise, and leads her forward : then he
kisses her hand, bowing over it with a very courtly air.

The Lady.   What am I, then ?

Pierrot.   A most divine Marquise !
Perhaps that attitude hath too much ease.

(Passes her.)

Ah, that is better !   To complete the plan,
Nothing is necessary save a fan.

The Lady.   Cool is the night, what needs it ?

Pierrot.   Madame, pray
Reflect, it is essential to our play.

The Lady.   (Taking a lily.)
Here is my fan !

Pierrot.   So, use it with intent :
The deadliest arm in beauty's armament !

The Lady.   What do we next ?

Pierrot.   We talk !

The Lady.   But what about ?

Pierrot.   We quiz the company and praise the rout ;
              Are polished, petulant, malicious, sly,
              Or what you will, so reputations die.
              Observe the Duchess in Venetian lace,
              With the red eminence.

The Lady.   A pretty face !

Pierrot.   For something tarter set thy wits to search—
              " She loves the churchman better than the church."

The Lady.   Her blush is charming ; would it were her own !

Pierrot.   Madame is merciless !

The Lady.   Is that the tone ?

Pierrot.   The very tone : I swear thou lackest naught.
              Madame was evidently bred at Court.

The Lady. Thou speakest glibly: 'tis not of thine age.

Pierrot. I listened much, as best becomes a page.

The Lady. I like thy Court but little——

Pierrot.   Hush! the Queen!
Bow, but not low—thou knowest what I mean.

The Lady. Nay, that I know not!

Pierrot.   Though she wear a crown,
'Tis from La Pompadour one fears a frown.

The Lady. Thou art a child: thy malice is a game.

Pierrot. A most sweet pastime—scandal is its name.

The Lady. Enough, it wearies me.

Pierrot.   Then, rare Marquise,
Desert the crowd to wander through the trees.

(He bows low, and she curtsies; they move round the
stage. When they pass before the Statue he seizes her
hand and falls on his knee.)

The Lady. What wouldst thou now?

Pierrot.   Ah, prithee, what, save thee!

The Lady. Was this included in thy comedy?

Pierrot. Ah, mock me not! In vain with quirk and jest
I strive to quench the passion in my breast;
In vain thy blandishments would make me play:
Still I desire far more than I can say.
My knowledge halts, ah, sweet, be piteous,
Instruct me still, while time remains to us,
Be what thou wist, Goddess, moon-maid, *Marquise*,
So that I gather from thy lips heart's ease,
Nay, I implore thee, think thee how time flies!

The Lady. Hush! I beseech thee, even now night dies.

Pierrot. Night, day, are one to me for thy soft sake.

(He entreats her with imploring gestures, she hesitates: then puts her finger on her lip, hushing him.)

The Lady. It is too late, for hark! the birds awake.

Pierrot. The birds awake! It is the voice of day!

The Lady. Farewell, dear youth! They summon me away.

(The light changes, it grows daylight: and music imitates the twitter of the birds. They stand gazing at the morning: then Pierrot sinks back upon his bed, he covers his face in his hands.)

The Lady.   (Bending over him.)

Music, my maids! His weary senses steep
In soft untroubled and oblivious sleep,
With mandragore anoint his tired eyes,
That they may open on mere memories,
Then shall a vision seem his lost delight,
With love, his lady for a summer's night.
Dream thou hast dreamt all this, when thou awake,
Yet still be sorrowful, for a dream's sake.
I leave thee, sleeper! Yea, I leave thee now,
Yet take my legacy upon thy brow:
Remember me, who was compassionate,

And opened for thee once, the ivory gate.
I come no more, thou shalt not see my face
When I am gone to mine exalted place :
Yet all thy days are mine, dreamer of dreams,
All silvered over with the moon's pale beams :
Go forth and seek in each fair face in vain,
To find the image of thy love again.
All maids are kind to thee, yet never one
Shall hold thy truant heart till day be done.
Whom once the moon has kissed, loves long and late,
Yet never finds the maid to be his mate.
Farewell, dear sleeper, follow out thy fate.

(The Moon Maiden withdraws : a song is sung from
behind : it is full day.)

THE MOON MAIDEN'S SONG.

Sleep! Cast thy canopy
    Over this sleeper's brain,
Dim grow his memory,
    When he awake again.

Love stays a summer night,
    Till lights of morning come ;

Then takes her wingèd flight
    Back to her starry home.

Sleep! Yet thy days are mine;
    Love's seal is over thee :
Far though my ways from thine,
    Dim though thy memory.

Love stays a summer night,
    Till lights of morning come ;
Then takes her winged flight
    Back to her starry home.

(When the song is finished, the curtain falls upon
Pierrot sleeping.)

THE END.

www.ingramcontent.com/pod-product-compliance
Lightning Source LLC
Chambersburg PA
CBHW061239260626
47172CB00003B/920